Teggs is no ... he's an **ASTROSAUR!** Captain of the amazing spaceship DSS *Sauropod*, he goes on dangerous missions and fights evil – along with his faithful crew, Gipsy, Arx and Iggy.

For more astro-fun visit the website www.astrosaurs.co.uk

EDENDERRY

1 0 DEC 2021

WITHDRAWN

D0262682

www.**kidsatrandomhouse**.co.uk

Read all the adventures of Teggs, Gipsy, Blink and Dutch at Astrosaurs Academy!

Find out more at www.astrosaurs.co.uk

Astrosaurs

THE CARNIVORE CURSE

Steve Cole

Illustrated by Woody Fox

RED FOX

THE CARNIVORE CURSE
A RED FOX BOOK 978 1 862 30256 3

First published in Great Britain by Red Fox,
an imprint of Random House Children's Books
A Random House Group Company

This edition published 2009

3 5 7 9 10 8 6 4 2

Text copyright © Steve Cole, 2009
Cover illustration and cards © Dynamo Design, 2009
Map © Charlie Fowkes, 2009
Illustrations copyright © Woody Fox, 2009

The right of Steve Cole to be identified as the author of this work
has been asserted in accordance with the Copyright, Designs and
Patents Act 1988.

All rights reserved. No part of this publication may be reproduced,
stored in a retrieval system, or transmitted in any form or by any
means, electronic, mechanical, photocopying, recording or otherwise,
without the prior permission of the publishers.

The Random House Group Limited supports the Forest Stewardship
Council (FSC), the leading international forest certification organization.
All our titles that are printed on Greenpeace-approved FSC-certified paper
carry the FSC logo. Our paper procurement policy can be found at
www.rbooks.co.uk/environment.

Typeset in Bembo Schoolbook by Palimpsest Book Production Limited,
Grangemouth, Stirlingshire

Red Fox Books are published by Random House Children's Books,
61–63 Uxbridge Road, London W5 5SA

www.**kids**at**random**house.co.uk
www.**rbooks**.co.uk

Addresses for companies within The Random House Group Limited can
be found at: www.randomhouse.co.uk/offices.htm

THE RANDOM HOUSE GROUP Limited Reg. No. 954009

A CIP catalogue record for this book is available from the British Library.

Printed in the UK by CPI Bookmarque, Croydon, CR0 4TD.

Class: _JF_
Acc: 11 | 9882
Inv: 11 | 295
£ S.70

To William and Martha

WARNING!

THINK YOU KNOW ABOUT DINOSAURS?

THINK AGAIN!

The dinosaurs . . .
   Big, stupid, lumbering reptiles. Right?
   All they did was eat, sleep and roar a bit. Right?
   Died out millions of years ago when a big meteor struck the Earth. Right?

Wrong!

The dinosaurs weren't stupid. They may have had small brains, but they used them well. They had big thoughts and big dreams.

By the time the meteor hit, the last dinosaurs had already left Earth for ever. Some breeds had discovered how to travel through space as early as the Triassic period, and were already enjoying a new life among the stars. No one has found evidence of dinosaur technology yet. But the first fossil bones were only unearthed in 1822, and new finds are being made all the time.

The proof is out there, buried in the ground.

And the dinosaurs live on, way out in space, even now. They've settled down in a place they call the Jurassic Quadrant and over the last sixty-five million years they've gone on evolving.

The dinosaurs we'll be meeting are

 part of a special
group called
the Dinosaur
Space Service.
Their job is to
explore space, to go on exciting
missions and to fight evil and protect
the innocent!

These heroic herbivores are not just
dinosaurs.

They are *astrosaurs*!

*NOTE: The following story has been
translated from secret Dinosaur Space Service
records. Earthling dinosaur names are used
throughout, although some changes have
been made for easy reading. There's even a
guide to help you pronounce the dinosaur
names on the next page.*

Talking Dinosaur!

How to say the prehistoric
names in this book . . .

STEGOSAURUS -
STEG-oh-SORE-us

HADROSAUR -
HAD-roh-sore

DIMORPHODON -
die-MORF-oh-don

IGUANODON -
ig-WA-noh-don

BARYONYX -
Bare-ee-ON-ix

TRICERATOPS -
try-SERRA-tops

SELLOSAURUS -
sel-oh-SORE-us

THE CREW OF THE DSS SAUROPOD

**CAPTAIN
TEGGS STEGOSAUR**

ARX ORANO,
FIRST OFFICER

GIPSY SAURINE,
COMMUNICATIONS
OFFICER

IGGY TOOTH,
CHIEF ENGINEER

Jurassic Quadrant

Ankylos

Steggos

Diplox

INDEPENDEN
DINOSAUR
ALLIANCE

vegetarian sector

**Squawk
Major**

DSS
UNION OF
PLANETS

PTEROSAURIA

Tri System

Corytho **Lambeos**

Iguanos

Aqua Minor

Geldos Cluster

Teerex Major

Olympus

TYRANNOSAUR
TERRITORIES

carnivore
sector

Raptos

Planet Sixty

THEROPOD EMPIRE

Megalos

Cryptos

vegmeat
zone
(neutral space)

SEA REPTILE
SPACE

Pliosaur
Nurseries

Not to scale

THE
CARNIVORE
CURSE

Chapter One

JOURNEY INTO FEAR

Captain Teggs Stegosaur sat in his control pit, chewing tensely on a twig. His amazing spaceship, the DSS *Sauropod* – finest craft in the Dinosaur Space Service – was zooming deeper into danger with every passing moment. Beads of sweat sat on Teggs's scaly orange-brown skin, and his ever-hungry tummy gave a nervous rumble.

"We are now five million miles inside the Carnivore Sector," reported Gipsy Saurine, the stripy hadrosaur in charge of the ship's communications. Her pretty face was creased in a frown. "Just think, there must be billions of meat-eating dinos all around us!"

Her words set off a chorus of squawks and squeals from the dimorphodon, the little flying reptiles that helped to work the *Sauropod*'s complicated controls. "All right, gang, don't get your wings in a wobble!" Teggs called to them. "Better keep thoughts like that to yourself, Gipsy."

"Sorry, Captain." Gipsy whistled to the dimorphodon and they settled down again. "But I really wish we were back in plant-eater space where we belong."

"*I* wish we knew more about our mission," growled Iggy Tooth, the *Sauropod's* Chief Engineer. The stocky iguanodon pointed at the scanner screen, which showed two pointed blood-red spacecraft flying alongside. "For instance, why we need to stay so close to those baryonyx battleships.

Nasty old rust-buckets – with even nastier old meat-eaters on board."

"Don't be rude about those baryonyx troops, Ig," Teggs told him. "If they weren't protecting us from all the *other* meat-eating trouble-makers out there, we'd be in real trouble!"

Gipsy sighed. "What a crazy situation."

And Teggs had to agree.

The *Sauropod* usually whizzed about the Vegetarian Sector of space, keeping peaceful plant-eating dinosaurs safe from hungry carnivore attacks. But right now, Teggs and his fellow astrosaurs were on a secret mission to *help* some of those carnivores. "We're taking a super-important dino-doctor to the baryonyx planet, Baronia," Teggs reflected. "But why?"

A green triceratops strode onto the flight deck. It was Arx – the *Sauropod*'s brainy first officer.

"Hello, Arx," said Iggy. "Been chatting with your new mate Doctor Herdlip, have you?"

"*Chatting*?" Arx frowned. "Herdlip is the biggest expert on space diseases in the galaxy, Iggy. He doesn't do chatting!"

"I suppose he's far too important and busy," said Teggs.

5

Arx nodded and sighed. "Shame, though – I'd love a good natter with Herdlip about space medicine! But he's locked himself away in my laboratory. I've been waiting by the door for ages, hoping he might come out."

"Never mind, Arx," said Gipsy. "I'm sure you'll both get a chance to talk on Baronia." Suddenly, she clutched her headphones. "Captain! Incoming message from Admiral Rosso."

"At last!" Teggs cried. Rosso was the crusty old barosaurus in charge of the DSS. "Perhaps now we'll get some answers."

Gipsy flicked a switch. The baryonyx ships faded from the scanner screen and Rosso's stern, wrinkly face appeared. "Ah, Teggs. You've almost reached your destination, so it should be safe to explain why you're needed so urgently."

Teggs saluted from his control pit. "What's happening on Baronia, sir?"

Rosso held up a picture of a grey baryonyx in regal robes, wearing a crown. Teggs shivered slightly. All baryonyx looked like giant gruesome crocodiles with hunched backs and long, narrow jaws full of pointed teeth – and the one in Rosso's picture looked scarier than most.

"This is King Jeck, the elderly ruler of the baryonyx," said Rosso. "Quite peaceful as carnivores go, but right now he's very sick. He has caught Ribchomper's Mump-Bumps."

"That's a nasty illness that only

affects meat-guzzling dinos in their old age," Arx noted. "It's sometimes called the Carnivore Curse. The older you are, the more dangerous it is."

"It could prove deadly to a meat-eater as old as King Jeck," said Rosso. "And Jeck's nephew – a vain, battle-hungry creature called Prince Poota – is next in line to the throne. He can't wait to take his uncle's crown and lead the baryonyx into battle against us plant-eaters."

"But why?" asked Gipsy.

"He wants to hang out with the most powerful carnivore rulers, like King Groosum the T. rex and the Raptor Royal," Arx noted. "But they won't take him seriously until he's started a war."

"Now I understand," Teggs told Rosso. "You want Jeck to get better so that he can stay king and keep things peaceful."

"And *that's* why we're bringing an expert in space diseases to Baronia!" Gipsy realized.

"Correct," said Rosso. "Doctor Herdlip believes he may have found a cure for the Mump-Bumps, and I have persuaded King Jeck to try it out. It's his only chance to pull through."

"But why is this all such a big secret?" asked Iggy.

"If it got about that a carnivore king was saved by some puny plant-eaters, there would be an uproar," Arx said. "King Jeck might be overthrown anyway!"

"Precisely," Rosso agreed. "Teggs, you must deliver Doctor Herdlip to Jeck's palace so that he can cure the king, and then get out again as quickly as possible. Good luck!"

The astrosaurs saluted. Rosso's image slowly faded from the scanner screen and the two blood-red battle cruisers reappeared. Teggs could see Baronia now, a red planet, growing larger as they approached.

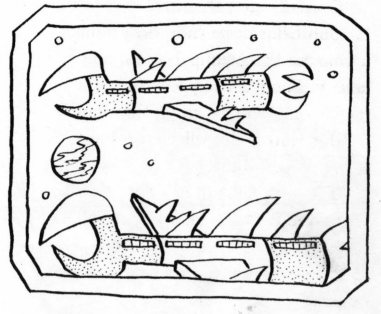

"No wonder Herdlip has locked himself in the lab," said Iggy. "He must still be tinkering with his cure."

Teggs nodded, "Arx, why don't you see if he needs any help before we land? That will give you a chance to talk to him!"

Arx saluted, smiled and hurried away.

As he left, one of Gipsy's controls bleeped. "Urgent message incoming from our baryonyx escorts," she reported, flicking a switch.

A roar burst from the *Sauropod's* speakers. "Plant-eaters, we are under attack! Prince Poota has—"

KA-BLAMMM! The *Sauropod* rocked as the nearest baryonyx battleship exploded into blazing pieces.

"Battle stations!" yelled Teggs.

The dimorphodon flapped to their posts. The lights dimmed. "Red alert!" screeched the alarm pterosaur, her shrill warning echoing throughout the *Sauropod*. "Danger! Under attack! *SQUAWWWK!*"

"No sign of enemy ships," said Iggy, studying the space radar.

KER-BOOOOM! The next moment, the *other* baryonyx battleship blew up in a blaze of light! The astrosaurs were thrown to the floor by the force of the blast.

The flock of dimorphodon helped Gipsy up. "What's happening?" she cried.

"You heard that poor baryonyx," Teggs shouted, leaping back into his control pit. "Prince Poota must have found out we're coming. He wants to make sure we don't cure King Jeck so he can start his crazy war!"

"And he's firing from somewhere on Baronia." Iggy pointed to the scanner. "Look!"

The red bulk of the baryonyx planet filled the screen and from its middle, a bright white ball of deadly laser-light was streaking from the planet's surface towards them ...

"Iggy, get us out of here!" Teggs shouted.

But it was too late. The laser blast hit, and the astrosaurs' yells were lost in an ear-splitting explosion . ..

Chapter Two

THE DUNG AND THE DANGER

Just a minute earlier, Arx had reached his lab on the *Sauropod*'s sixth level when the warning screech of the alarm pterosaur broke the silence.

"Doctor Herdlip?" he shouted through the lab door. "It's Arx. Open up, quickly! I'm not sure what's happening, but I'll make sure you're safe—"

Suddenly, the ship was smashed sideways as if it had been knocked over by a giant, and Arx gasped as he was hurled into the nearest wall. The sound of breaking glass and clattering beakers came from the lab – along with a howl of dismay from Herdlip.

"He must be hurt," Arx muttered. Summoning all his strength he charged across the tilting corridor, lowered his head and smashed down the lab door. It was smoky and smelly inside, and broken equipment crunched under Arx's heavy feet. "Doctor Herdlip," he called from the doorway, "are you all right?"

For a moment, nothing stirred. Then Herdlip came waddling out in a stained lab coat. He was a purple sellosaurus the size of a Shetland pony, with a long neck, a stripy tail and a face like a startled tortoise. "Oh, dear! Oh, help!" he squealed. "What a to-do!"

Arx frowned. "You're dripping wet."

"That blast covered me in chemicals!" squeaked Dr Herdlip. He pulled off his wet jacket and hurled it back inside the smoky room. "Nothing to worry about, I'm sure. But I really must have a shower at once!"

"A shower?" cried Arx as the *Sauropod* shook again. "But we're under attack!"

"Under attack?" Herdlip gulped. "Then I think I'll go to the lavatory too while I'm there!" He dashed away towards the toilet block. "Good day!"

With a helpless shrug, Arx pelted back to the flight deck. The emergency lights were flickering and the

dimorphodon flapped about, burning
their beaks on the sparking controls.
Teggs, Iggy and Gipsy were sprawled
upside down in the control pit.

Quickly, Arx helped Iggy and Gipsy
climb out. "What hit us?"

"A laser blast from Baronia," Iggy
groaned. "Strong enough to shatter our
shields."

"Where's Doctor Herdlip?" asked Teggs, now Iggy's bottom was out of his face. "Is he OK?"

"Er, he's having a shower," said Arx. "I think he might be in shock. I don't suppose he's seen many space battles."

Gipsy frowned. "If that laser hits us again with the shields down, we won't see many more ourselves!"

"Then we must make sure it doesn't." Teggs chewed heroically on a squashed fern. "Arx, can we trace the blast back to its source?"

Arx was already at his post. "I'll lock our dung torpedoes onto the exact location now, Captain."

"Sensors detect energy build-up on the planet surface," Iggy warned them. "Whoever's down there, they're getting ready to shoot again."

"Fire *all* dung torpedoes, Arx," Teggs shouted. "We must zap that weapon — *now!*"

Arx whacked the fire button with his nose-horn. "Torpedoes fired!"

Gipsy gasped. "But the laser blast has just fired too."

"They'll meet each other head-on," Iggy realized.

"White hot light against supercharged dung . . . I wonder which will win?" Teggs leaned forward in his control pit. "Let's get down there fast!"

The *Sauropod* zoomed through the murky skies towards the source of the blasts. On the scanner screen they saw a white explosion flare up near the surface of Baronia, closely followed by a huge splurge of brown. And as they broke through the clouds, the astrosaurs saw a massive metal cannon pointing up from a wasteland below. It was scorched black and bunged up with fresh, steaming dung.

"Clearly the force of the laser blast exploded our dung torpedoes," Arx concluded. "The resulting thick layer of dung reflected the power back at the gun and then clogged its workings."

"In other words, *WA-HEYY!*"

cheered Iggy. "That laser won't be destroying any more spaceships."

"Captain," called Gipsy urgently. "Video message incoming from King Jeck's palace."

"Put it on the scanner," ordered Teggs.

The image of a dark-blue baryonyx appeared. "I am Palace Guard Captain Griffen," croaked the frightening figure. He had yellow, staring eyes and big gaps in his broken teeth. "We apologize for your near-destruction, plant-eaters. The ground-to-space laser-cannon was operated by agents of Prince Poota."

"We thought as much," said Teggs.

"The agents were seen as they fled from your downpour of dung," Griffen went on. "But we have not yet caught them."

Gipsy gulped. "So they might try again."

"Correct," snarled Griffen. "You will

proceed to the Palace at once and park in the Royal Gardens. Do *not* emerge until my guards come to fetch you, or Prince Poota may attack again." He narrowed his yellow eyes. "That is all."

The screen went dark, and Iggy frowned. "Nice to feel welcome, isn't it?"

"Stuck on a planet of carnivores," sighed Gipsy.

Arx nodded. "At least until Doctor Herdlip cures King Jeck."

"I wish I didn't have to!" twittered a high voice behind them. They turned to find Herdlip in a dressing gown, soaking wet, at the back of the flight deck. "If you ask me,

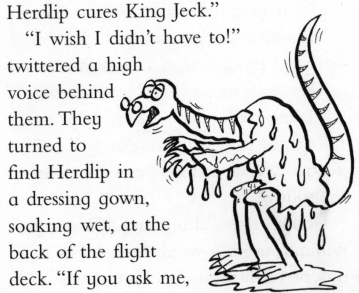

24

the baryonyx are *all* sick. War-loving carnivore loopers!"

"A lot of them just got blown up while trying to protect you," Teggs reminded him sternly.

Arx quickly changed the subject. "Did you enjoy your shower, Doctor Herdlip?"

"Eh? Oh, yes. It was, er, very wet." The sellosaurus cleared his throat. "Now, I want a cleaning robot to help me clear up the lab."

"I'll help, if you like," Arx offered.

"*No!*" Dr Herdlip snapped. "In unskilled hands, my lotions and medicines could be highly dangerous. It's robots or nothing."

"Then I'm afraid it's nothing," said Teggs. "We only have dinosaur cleaners on board."

Herdlip scowled and hurried away without another word. Arx's horns drooped a little.

"Don't worry, Arx," said Gipsy. "He's probably just a bit shaken up."

"Let's hope Prince Poota doesn't try to shake us up even more," said Iggy.

"Well, with any luck, Griffen's guards are as scary as he is." Teggs smiled ruefully. "Then Poota's agents won't *dare* come near us!"

Iggy chuckled, and Gipsy smiled as the *Sauropod* flew off towards the palace. But Arx could only frown. Something in his bones told him that the danger was far from over. That, if anything, it had barely begun . . .

Chapter Three

THE REPULSIVE PALACE

Once the *Sauropod* had landed, Arx and Iggy started repairing its shields.

Herdlip cleaned up the lab, then locked himself in his room.

Teggs, Gipsy and the dimorphodon waited on the flight deck.

Many hours passed, but Guard Captain Griffen did not call.

"What's keeping him?" Gipsy complained. "Don't the baryonyx want their king to be cured?"

Teggs sighed and ate his fiftieth clump of ferns. "Perhaps they've had another run-in with Prince Poota."

Suddenly, a loud beep told them a

message was coming through. The
dimorphodon turned on the scanner
and Griffen's dark, scary head appeared
on the screen.

"Captain Teggs," he hissed, "my
guards have now surrounded your ship.
They will take you and Doctor Herdlip
to the royal palace. No one else."

Gipsy frowned. "Why can't the rest
of us come?"

"Two are easier to protect than many," Griffen growled. "I have already lost enough troops because of you!" The screen went blank.

"He's got a point, Gipsy." Teggs sighed. "Call Herdlip and tell him to meet me at the main doors in five minutes." As Teggs bounced over to the lift, he saw that Gipsy looked worried. "It's all right, I'll take good care of him."

She managed a small smile. "And yourself, please!"

Five minutes later, Teggs was standing by the *Sauropod*'s main doors. Herdlip stood nervously beside him. He was

holding a large suitcase full of medical
supplies, and gulped when Teggs
opened the main doors.

Night had fallen on Baronia. Three yellow moons hung in a sky the colour of old scabs. The gardens were grotty and overgrown, and the smell of sewage filled Teggs's nostrils as he gazed at King Jeck's palace. It was like something out of a horror film – a huge castle littered with spooky towers and turrets. Blood-red ivy climbed the crumbling walls.

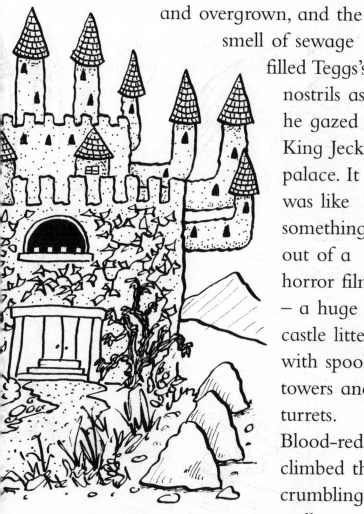

"Move!" grunted Griffen, and four of his baryonyx guards bundled Teggs and Herdlip towards the nightmarish building.

"Is King Jeck ready for his medicine?" asked Herdlip nervously.

"No." Griffen opened a big bronze door in the palace wall and pushed the plant-eaters inside. "He is sleeping. His orders were that he must not be disturbed."

Teggs frowned. "I thought he needed treatment at once?"

"No one may question King Jeck," growled Griffen, leading

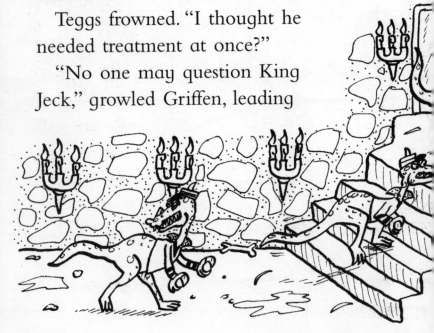

them down a dark, winding corridor, lit by flickering candles. "However, I have prepared bedrooms here for you both, so you can treat him the moment he wakes."

"How lovely," muttered Herdlip.

The astrosaurs and their guards walked in uneasy silence through the gloomy stone passageways. They passed a very large, smelly kitchen

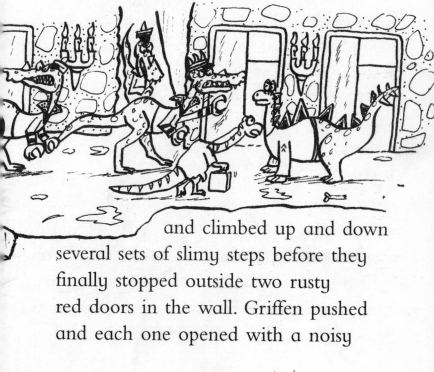

and climbed up and down several sets of slimy steps before they finally stopped outside two rusty red doors in the wall. Griffen pushed and each one opened with a noisy squeak of their hinges.

"Stay in your rooms and lock the doors," he told the two plant-eaters. "A guard will wait outside. You will be woken when His Majesty is ready."

"Not exactly the five-star Ferns Hotel," Teggs muttered. The rooms were full of cobwebs and earwigs and half-chewed bones. A grimy window overlooked the tangled gardens. A bed of damp straw lay in the corner beside a very large and mucky toilet. "Er, which room would you like, Doctor Herdlip?"

But the sellosaurus simply stepped

inside the nearest room and slammed
the door behind him. Teggs heard
heavy bolts being drawn across, and
shrugged. "OK – good night to you
too!"

Griffen and three of the guards
stamped away without another word.
The remaining baryonyx eyed Teggs
coldly. Teggs winked at him, yawned
and went inside. "I'm so tired I could
fall asleep in a skonk-skuggler's
armpit!" he declared, curling up on the
damp floor. "Mind you, even a skonk-
skuggler's *bottom* would smell better
than this dump . . ."

Despite the stink, Teggs was soon
asleep. But he didn't stay that way for
long. Minutes later, the sound of a
terrifying roar outside woke him with
a start.

"I don't think much of the royal
alarm clocks!" said Teggs, rubbing his
sleepy eyes. He quickly ran outside –

and found the guard sprawled asleep on
the floor with a rusty red door on top
of him. "Hmm. Either baryonyx guards
like very uncomfortable bed covers,
or . . . " Teggs spun round and, sure
enough, found that Dr Herdlip's door
had been torn off its hinges! Bottles,
beakers and test tubes lay broken on
the floor. The window was smashed and
the bed had been torn apart and
shoved down the toilet. But Herdlip
himself was nowhere to be seen.

He had vanished!

Chapter Four

MONSTER ON THE LOOSE

"Sound the alarm!" Teggs cried, shaking the guard. "Fetch Griffen!"

"What hit me?" groaned the baryonyx guard.

"That's what I have to find out," said Teggs, grimly. While the guard stumbled off to alert Captain Griffen, Teggs charged along the corridor in search of Herdlip.

As he skidded down the slimy steps he heard a commotion from the smelly kitchens up ahead. He peered in, and gasped – the place had been trashed! A fridge lay upside down. The walls were splattered with squashed fish. A panic-stricken baryonyx in a chef's hat was prancing about with a large rolling pin. Two more cooks were struggling out from under a huge overturned table.

"What happened?" Teggs demanded.

"I've never seen anything like it!" cried the chef, wide-eyed with shock. "A huge monster just barged in!"

Teggs frowned. "A *monster*?"

The chef nodded. "It tore open the fridge, chomped down a ton of meat, threw a table at my slaves—"

"And chucked raw fish everywhere,"

Teggs interrupted. "Yes, I can see."

"Actually, the fish was already there," the chef informed him. "It's an air freshener – some of my meals stink!"

Teggs rolled his eyes. "Did you get a good look at this monster? Was it carrying a sellosaurus under one arm, by any chance?"

"I didn't see it clearly," the baryonyx confessed. "I was trying to hide in a cupboard." He frowned. "Hey, what's a plant-eater doing around here anyway?"

"Staying off the menu!" said Teggs firmly. "Bye!" He sprinted back out of the kitchens and down the winding passages until he reached a crossroads. "Which way did this monster go?" he muttered.

Then he heard a faint, muffled voice calling from somewhere up ahead, "*Help! Help me!*"

"I'm coming!" Teggs shouted, dashing

off again into the gloom. But as he turned a corner he tripped over something large and scaly. "*OOF!*"

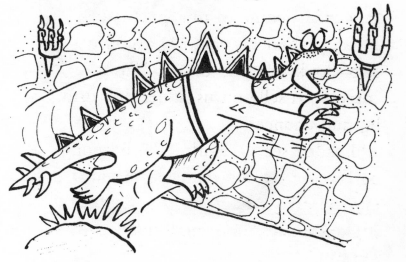

"Captain Teggs?" came a familiar twittering voice. "Is that you?"

"Doctor Herdlip?" Teggs struggled up. To his surprise and delight – there was the little sellosaurus, sitting in a daze in the middle of the passage. "What happened? Are you all right?"

Herdlip rubbed his head dizzily. "The answer to both questions is, 'I'm not entirely sure'!"

Suddenly, footsteps sounded behind them. It was Griffen, looking puzzled and angry. "I warned you to stay in your rooms."

"Doctor Herdlip didn't have much choice!" Teggs retorted. "A monster broke into his room and kidnapped him."

"The guard only saw a door flying towards him," Griffen growled. "But the king's chef was raving about a monster when I passed the kitchens—"

"*Help!*" came the same distant cry as before.

"Come on, Griffen," said Teggs, dashing onwards down the passage. "Perhaps we'll see the monster for ourselves!" He came to a door and

threw it open to reveal a gloomy
storeroom. Three baryonyx were inside,
wrestling with a small, struggling figure
bundled up in a heavy red blanket.

"*Help!*" the figure croaked again. But
the biggest baryonyx whacked it with
his tail, and it stopped moving.

Griffen barged past Teggs and
addressed the biggest baryonyx.
"What's going on, Sergeant Donkle?"
He frowned at the figure hidden
beneath the blanket. "Have you caught
the monster?"

"*Monster?*" Donkle frowned. "No, sir, this is a thief – one of Prince Poota's lot. He was trying to pinch some weapons, probably wanted to use them against King Jeck."

"Aha!" Griffen nodded knowingly. "This so-called *monster* was a trick to distract us while the thief did his work. Which means Poota's rabble have got into the palace." He scowled. "Take that traitor to the dungeon, Donkle, then organize a search."

"But be careful," Teggs added. "Whoever snatched Doctor Herdlip is incredibly powerful."

Just then, Herdlip himself waddled up, clutching a pen and paper. "Captain Teggs,

that m-m-monster thing smashed all my medical supplies," he cried. "I-I will need more." He held out a piece of paper. "Please fetch these things from your ship at once."

"All this?" Teggs stared at the scrawls on the paper in surprise. "It would take three dinosaurs to carry that lot!"

"I cannot spare any guards," said Griffen gruffly. "They are all needed to search the palace."

"No problemo!" Teggs pulled out his communicator and winked at Dr Herdlip. "I know just the three dinosaurs we need . . ."

Thirty minutes later, as dawn broke
slowly over Baronia, Iggy, Arx and
Gipsy staggered up to the palace with
boxes of lotions, potions and pills. Teggs
and Griffen met them at the door.

"Nice pad," said Iggy, looking round.
"*Not!*"

Griffen glared at him. "I did not ask
you to come here," he rasped. "You
stay in this palace at your own risk."
With that he stomped off, his long blue
nose in the air. Gipsy made a rude
face behind his back.

Arx could barely hold up the heavy crate he was carrying. "Why does Doctor Herdlip need so many chemicals, Captain? He's used up all our medical supplies!"

"I don't know," Teggs admitted, taking a box from Gipsy. "I'll explain what's been happening on the way in . . ."

By the time Teggs had told his story, the astrosaurs had reached the wreck of Herdlip's room. Gipsy, Iggy and Arx shivered when they saw what the monster had done. Herdlip himself was shut away inside Teggs's old room, with two baryonyx guarding the door. They stepped grumpily aside as Teggs approached.

"Doctor Herdlip?" Teggs called. "We've brought your supplies."

Herdlip threw open the door. "Bring them inside," he ordered. "Quickly! Immediately! *Now!*"

Iggy frowned. "All right, keep your scales on."

Arx shot him a look. "Doctor Herdlip is under a lot of strain, Iggy." He put down his own crate beside Teggs's and Gipsy's. "He's got to mix his cure for Ribchomper's Mump-Bumps again from scratch."

"Eh? What?" Herdlip was already busily sorting through the boxes. "Really, I can't concentrate with you all hovering. Please go away!"

Frowning, the astrosaurs did as he asked. Herdlip slammed the door after them, and the baryonyx guards stepped back into place.

"Not even a thank you," fumed Gipsy.

"Never mind him," said Teggs. "I want to know where that monster went. I hate unsolved mysteries."

Arx nodded. "*I'd* like to know how Poota's agents smuggled the monster into the palace without anyone seeing."

"Why don't you ask the thief caught in the storeroom?" Gipsy suggested. "He must know something."

"Too late," snarled Griffen, charging

up the passage towards them with Donkle and a dozen guards. "I've just been to question that traitor myself. But he has vanished into thin air — just like that monster of yours. The dungeon is empty!"

"What?" Teggs frowned. "How?"

"There is only one explanation." Donkle's eyes narrowed. "You plant-eaters helped him escape!"

"That's ridiculous!" Gipsy spluttered. "We've only been here a few minutes."

"Don't try to trick me!" Griffen bellowed. He turned to Teggs, "You and Herdlip smashed up the room *and* the cure for King Jeck, didn't you? Then you blamed it on this ridiculous made-up creature."

"That's not true!" Teggs protested.

"And while my guards were busy hunting something that didn't exist, your friends sneakily set free our prisoner." Griffen bared his broken teeth. "I think you are all agents of Poota!"

"What a *load* of poo-ta!" Iggy shouted back.

Teggs nodded. "We came here in peace—"

"But you will leave here in *pieces*!" hissed Griffen. "Get them, guards!"

The astrosaurs braced themselves as the drooling gang of carnivores closed in . . .

Chapter Five

THE KING AND THE CURE

"Come on, guys," Teggs told the guards calmly. "I know you're all fed up, but please – don't do something *we* might regret!"

Griffen's troops made disgusting, slobbery noises as they advanced on the astrosaurs. Arx lowered his head ready to charge, and Iggy and Gipsy struck dino-judo poses. Teggs

flexed his powerful tail and prepared to fight.

But suddenly, a small, skinny baryonyx came running up to Griffen, out of breath. "It is I, the king's slave," he panted. "I bring a vital message from the royal bedchamber!"

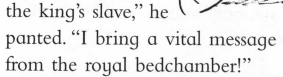

"Wait," Griffen told his guards, and they reluctantly obeyed as he turned to the newcomer. "Is the king awake?"

The skinny baryonyx nodded sadly. "I hardly recognized him this morning. So lumpy and bumpy, he can barely speak . . ."

"Sounds like he's reached the final stages of the Carnivore Curse," said Arx. "At his age, he can't last much longer."

"He needs the cure." Teggs looked at

Griffen. "I promise you, the only reason we're here is to help your king."

Suddenly, Herdlip burst out of his room clutching his battered white case. "Did somebody say the king was awake?" He  looked pale, blinking in alarm at the slobbering crowd of baryonyx. "I-I have just this moment mixed up a fresh batch of the cure."

"That was quick." Donkle stared at him suspiciously. "How do we know it isn't poison?"

"Why would we come all this way to poison a dying dinosaur?" Arx retorted.

"Very well," said Griffen slowly. "You may treat the king."

"At last!" Herdlip whispered. "The historic moment has arrived . . ."

"And if we *do* cure him, Griffen," said Teggs, "I want your promise that we can all leave Baronia unchewed!"

"Very well," Griffen grumbled. "Teggs, Herdlip, come with me. Donkle, lock up the others. I will question them later."

Donkle saluted. "In the meantime I'll keep searching for the escaped prisoner."

"See you soon," Teggs called to his crew as he and Herdlip were marched away by Griffen and the slave.

Donkle shoved Iggy, Arx and Gipsy into Herdlip's room and shut the door. The air smelled sharp and smoky, even with the window open. Bubbling beakers and foaming test tubes had been jammed into cracks in the floor or clamped into metal stands.

"This place looks like a mad-scientist's lab," said Iggy. "But I must say, old Herdlip is a fast worker, isn't he? I can't believe how quickly he whipped up a new cure for the Mump-Bumps!"

"Neither can I," said Arx gravely. "I read the secret files on his cure while we were stuck on the *Sauropod*. It would take at least a couple of hours to concoct – and he wouldn't need half these chemicals."

"Then . . . what *does* he need them for?" wondered Gipsy.

They looked at each other. But not one of them could think of the answer.

Teggs followed Griffen, Herdlip and the king's slave to the royal bedchamber. Herdlip trembled as he waddled along. *I'm not surprised he's nervous*, thought Teggs.

Soon, they reached some golden double doors. The slave banged a gong that stood beside them. "Your Majesty!" he squeaked. "The plant-eaters are here to make you well again!"

"Mmm-rrrrhb-nn'omp," came a muffled growl from within.

The doors slid open to reveal a grand room filled with ancient furniture, dimly lit by a dozen small candles. A whiff of mouldy pies and dirty pants filled the smoky air. But Teggs's eyes were quickly drawn to the big bed in the middle of the floor. The baryonyx king lay there, barely visible beneath a pile of blankets and hot-water bottles – three of which were perched on his head in place of a crown!

"Bow down to King Jeck," hissed Griffen. Teggs and Herdlip did as he asked.

"I have brought the cure for your ills," said Herdlip, holding up his white case.

"Gllph-rrhb," said King Jeck.

Herdlip took out a small pillbox and a flask full of pink liquid. "Take the

two tablets and wash them down with this special herbal drink, Your Majesty." The doctor's hands shook as he laid the offerings on the king's bed. "I guarantee that you will soon be feeling like a new dinosaur!"

"Urp," the king croaked, and turned his back on them all.

"King Jeck would like you to leave," the slave declared.

Griffen bowed so low his nose

scraped the floor, then he retreated from the room. Herdlip waddled after him and Teggs followed quickly, glad of the fresher air once the golden doors slid shut.

"Is it always so dark and smoky in there?" Teggs wondered.

Griffen shook his head sadly. "King Jeck has truly changed. How long before he recovers?"

"Ooh, not long." Herdlip smiled faintly. "Give it a couple of days and you won't believe the change in him."

"Well," grunted Griffen. "Until I see it for myself and find out more about this monster, you plant-eaters will stay here as my prisoners."

"Eh?" Herdlip looked alarmed. "Oh!"

"Perhaps it's just as well." Teggs patted him on the back. "After all, we've only just brought all those chemicals and medicines here!"

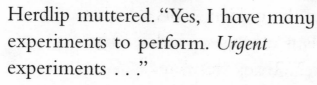

"Oh, yes," Herdlip muttered. "Yes, I have many experiments to perform. *Urgent* experiments . . ."

Soon, they reached Herdlip's room. The moment the door was unlocked, Iggy, Gipsy and Arx bounded outside, full of questions about what had

happened. While Teggs tried to answer them, Herdlip quietly slipped inside and bolted the door. "Silence, plant-eaters!" roared

Griffen. "It is *my* questions you must answer . . . in the dungeon! I intend to find out all you know about Poota's plans *and* his missing agent."

"That won't take long," said Gipsy. "Because we don't know anything!"

"But if Donkle had only questioned that prisoner instead of clobbering him, we would *all* know a lot more!" said Teggs crossly. "Such as, where is the monster that kidnapped Doctor Herdlip right now—"

Behind him, the wall suddenly exploded in a storm of flying stone and dust. The two baryonyx guards were hurled against Arx and Iggy, who in turn crashed into Griffen and Gipsy.

Only Teggs was left standing – he barely felt the bits of brickwork bouncing off his skin. He was too busy staring in horror at the colossal carnivore-creature climbing out through the hole in the wall. It was green and powerful with a spiky head and enormous slavering jaws. Six stone-shredding claws poked out of each hand. Raw hunger burned in the beast's piercing red eyes as it loomed over him . . .

"So *there* it is." Teggs gulped. "The monster!"

Chapter Six

SOMETHING IN THE SEWER

The creature ignored Griffen and the guards and lunged for Teggs! Thinking fast, he grabbed a large lump of stone and shoved it into the monster's mouth. Spluttering with anger, the monster lashed out with its tail and smashed Teggs backwards into the wall opposite. He landed in a dazed heap as the towering beast lurched towards him.

"Leave him alone!" cried Iggy. He tried to shoulder-charge the carnivore but it shrugged him off, spat out the stone and clamped its jaws around Iggy's tail instead. "Ow! Leave *me* alone too!" Struggling fiercely, Iggy felt the creature's teeth began to sink into his tough scaly hide . . .

"*NOOOOOO!*" hooted Gipsy loudly, still sprawled on the floor.

The monster stopped. It looked hard at Gipsy.

Suddenly, it spat out Iggy with a defiant roar. Then it turned and stamped away along the corridor, knocking Arx, Griffen and the baryonyx guards aside.

Teggs staggered over to Iggy. "Are you OK?"

"Just some scratches." Iggy smiled weakly. "I guess I was too tough and chewy for Big-Jaws there to bother with!"

Arx smiled at Gipsy as he helped her up. "Or else Gipsy's super-hoot shocked him into dropping you!"

Teggs looked at Griffen. "*Now* do you believe me about the monster?"

Griffen cuffed his two guards round the ears. "Don't just sit there," he shouted. "Get reinforcements and catch that creature!" They scuttled away dizzily.

"I've never seen anything like that before," said Iggy.

"It must be a specially trained pet of Prince Poota's," Griffen snarled.

Gipsy shuddered. "He should keep it on a lead!"

"I suppose the monster doesn't know that Doctor Herdlip has already given King Jeck the cure, and it's still trying to stop him," Arx reasoned.

"Captain!" said Gipsy urgently, peering through the hole in the wall. "Where's Herdlip gone?"

Teggs clambered into the doctor's room and peered round. Just like before, the experiments had been smashed and overturned as if a terrible struggle had

taken place. "Perhaps he jumped out through the window?" Teggs said. "It's broken like everything else."

"It's a long way down," Arx observed. "But the monster certainly must have got in that way. After all, the door's still locked!"

"There *is* one other place it might have come from," said Iggy, pointing to the shattered toilet. "From down there – maybe it crawled up the pipes!"

Gipsy gasped. "Perhaps its lair is in the sewers!"

Teggs nodded gravely. "That would explain why we couldn't find the monster before."

"It might have stashed Doctor Herdlip down there too!" said Iggy.

Teggs turned to Griffen. "I think we should split up and make *two* searches for Herdlip and the monster. Gipsy and I will join your guards searching the palace and the gardens, while Arx and Iggy check out the sewers."

Iggy looked at Arx. "Lucky us."

"*Mucky* us," Arx corrected him.

"We must move quickly," hissed

Griffen. "Like Prince Poota, this monster must be stopped!"

Iggy pulled a torch from his belt. "Geroni-*looooooooooooo*!" He jumped down the toilet. Holding his nose, Arx hopped down behind him.

Teggs, Gipsy and Griffen jogged along the gloomy stone corridors in anxious silence. They soon passed the kitchens. Teggs found the fridge upside down again and the chef hiding back in his cupboard. Only this time, even the dead fish on the walls had been scraped off.

"It ate *everything*!" wailed the quailing chef. "Even the mouldy rat that was holding open the window!"

71

"The monster's still hungry," Teggs realized. "So why didn't it eat Iggy when it had the chance?"

Suddenly, Donkle came scuttling up to Griffen. "We've found that monster, sir. It's rampaging about on Level Three."

Griffen's eyes lit up. "That's near the dungeons. Perhaps we can lock it inside."

Donkle gulped. "Um . . . Is that wise, sir?"

Teggs nodded. "The last prisoner you locked in there escaped straight away!"

"This time there will be no mistakes," vowed Griffen, pushing Donkle on ahead. And as Teggs and Gipsy followed, they hoped fervently that the captain was right . . .

Far below, Arx and Iggy were sloshing through the stinky sewers.

Iggy pointed his torch round with keen interest. "There's enough dung down here to run the *Sauropod*'s engines for a month!"

"I'm not carrying any of it back," Arx warned him. Then he sighed. "I hope we find Doctor Herdlip soon. He was up to something with those extra chemicals, I'm sure of it."

"Perhaps the monster thought so too," said Iggy. "That's why it smashed those experiments . . ." Suddenly, he stopped. "Hey. I think I heard something."

Arx froze, straining to hear. A low, quiet moan echoed eerily from the shadows up ahead.

"*Help . . . Please . . .*"

"Perhaps it's Doctor Herdlip!" Arx whispered. "Come on!"

The two astrosaurs bravely waded through the slimy muck towards the sound of the voice. Iggy's torch beam picked out something lying on a narrow ledge above the muck, bundled up in a heavy red blanket.

The bundle wriggled. "*Help*," the hoarse croak came again. "*Let me out!*"

"That doesn't sound like Herdlip." Iggy swallowed hard. "I've got a bad feeling about this."

Slowly, holding his breath, Arx

reached out one hand and yanked
back the blanket . . .

Chapter Seven

THE TERRIBLE TRUTH

Teggs could hear the distant shrieks of the monster getting closer as he and Gipsy followed Griffen and Donkle to the dungeons. The sound made him shiver.

Finally, the group reached a large, grim, forbidding metal door, which Griffen unlocked with a spiky red key. The dungeons beyond were damp, cold and smelly. Dim lights in the ceiling flickered on as they entered to reveal rusty manacles hanging from the blood-stained walls. Wet straw and bleached bones were scattered about the floor.

"How did your prisoner escape from this place?" Teggs wondered, looking inside.

"Dunno," Donkle snarled. "I clobbered the guard on duty. He hasn't woken up yet."

"Very good, Sergeant Donkle," said Griffen approvingly.

"It's *not* good, it's dumb!" Teggs banged his tail against the wall in frustration. "If you lot would only ask questions instead of hitting things—"

"Captain!" Gipsy interrupted, rushing over. "Look, where *you* hit something – the wall . . ."

Teggs swung round to find a couple of stones had fallen out. "The bricks are all loose!" He pulled out several more to reveal a dark space that smelled of dung. "You know, I might have just found a secret way out."

Griffen frowned. "*What?*"

"Shhhh," hissed Gipsy. "I can hear something moving on the other side!"

They all jumped as the loose stones

in the wall were suddenly smashed away and a sturdy, slightly smelly triceratops stepped into the dungeons.

"It's Arx!" Teggs stared in amazement. "But that means this secret way out leads to the sewer!"

"Correct, Captain." Arx nodded grimly. "And look who we found down there . . ."

Iggy stepped through the wall behind Arx, carrying a frail figure in his arms. It was an elderly baryonyx wrapped up in a blanket. His grey, wrinkled skin was covered in nasty lumps and bumps. He looked very unwell, but there was still a look of defiance in his watery eyes.

"What? *No!*" Griffen spluttered like he'd swallowed an electric bee. "It's really you . . . Your Majesty!"

"The *real* King Jeck," Arx agreed.

Teggs gasped. "Then . . . the one Herdlip treated in the royal bedroom was an imposter?"

"Not just any old imposter," croaked King Jeck furiously. "That baryonyx you thought was me was my nasty nephew – *Prince Poota himself!*"

Griffen looked as though he might explode. "*POOTA?* Here in the palace? Pretending to be king?"

"His agents fired the giant laser-cannon at the plant-eaters' ship to create a distraction," King Jeck explained. "While you and your guards dealt with that danger, Poota sneaked into the palace, hid me down here, turned my royal bedchamber into his secret base – and impersonated me."

"So Doctor Herdlip would give his cure to the wrong baryonyx!" Teggs realized. "Poota kept the lights down low, didn't speak and hid under blankets and hot-water bottles."

Griffen sighed. "I *said* the king seemed a changed dinosaur!"

"But why go to such trouble?" asked Gipsy. "I don't mean to be rude, Your Majesty, but why didn't he just squish you?"

"Poota is unpopular with the

baryonyx people," Jeck went on. "If they thought he had squished me, they would never accept him as their king. But if he could blame my death on you plant-eaters . . . pretend that your cure was a deadly poison . . ."

"Of course," said Arx glumly. "We came here in secret because you asked us to. But he could tell the people we came to attack your world."

"He even has proof," Iggy realized. "We blew up that laser-cannon – our dung torpedoes are plastered all over it!"

"Your Majesty, forgive me for my blindness." Griffen bowed so low that he

almost did a headstand. "But *how* could Poota and his agents get past my guards and move freely inside the palace?"

"Because of *him*!" Jeck pointed a long claw at Donkle. "That miserable worm is secretly working for my nasty nephew."

Donkle had been edging nervously towards the dungeon door. But now Arx quickly charged across and blocked his escape. "That's far enough, traitor," the triceratops growled.

"Last night I managed to escape from Poota's clutches," Jeck whispered – every word seemed an effort. "I tried to warn you all, but Donkle found me first. He hid me in this blanket, thumped me on the head to stop me talking and made out that *I* was one of Poota's agents."

Teggs understood. "Then he hid you behind the dungeon wall and told everyone you'd escaped."

King Jeck nodded weakly but his eyes had flickered shut. He was barely breathing now.

"He's in the very last stage of the Mump-Bumps," said Arx sadly. "The king needs Doctor Herdlip's special tablets to cure him."

"And the special herbal drink,"

84

Teggs reminded him. "Herdlip said it was vital."

Arx shook his head. "According to his secret notes, there's no drink needed. Just two tablets."

"It hardly matters now, does it?" Griffen stormed up to the trembling Donkle. "And it's all *your* fault! You dung-swallowing drudge-dog!" In a fury, he bashed the big guard on the head with his tail. Donkle went cross-eyed and flopped to the floor.

"Griffen," groaned Teggs. "I told you, hitting people is never the answer when you *need* answers! Such as, what does Donkle know about that monster? How does it figure in Poota's plans? What's it after?"

But even as he spoke, the monster's ear-splitting roar sounded from just outside. "I think it's after *us*!" said Arx, backing away from the door.

Gipsy's head-crest flushed neon blue in alarm as the monster came crashing into the dungeons. Its green spiky head swung this way and that, and its crimson eyes blazed. It released a triumphant, bellowing howl . . .

"Griffen, get Jeck to safety," Teggs commanded. The blue baryonyx nodded and took the king from Iggy. "Arx, lead them back through the sewers to Herdlip's room in case he's gone back there – he might be able to help. The rest of us will try to hold off the monster."

Griffen stared at Teggs. "You would risk your lives for a carnivore king?"

Teggs gave him a crooked smile. "That's why we came in the first place."

Arx saluted his captain, then ducked back into the hole in the wall. Clutching Jeck close, Griffen followed him.

The monster howled again. "All right, guys," said Teggs. "It's time to show this thing some plant-eater power!"

"Wait," cried Gipsy. "Something's happening!"

She was right. The carnivore froze for a moment. Then its claws flew to its neck. It started to cough, as if it had a Triassic frog in its throat. With every cough the creature seemed to grow a little smaller. Teggs and his friends stared in astounded silence as the monster screeched and steamed and

spluttered. Its spiky head grew
smoother and sleeker. The fangs
vanished and the fierce claws melted
away – the once-mighty monster
became a small, purple and very
familiar dinosaur . . .

"I don't believe it!" squeaked Iggy.
"The monster we've all been after –
it's *Doctor Herdlip*!"

Chapter Eight

THE MONSTER'S MISSION

Teggs stared in shock at Dr Herdlip. "The monster didn't kidnap you at all . . . it *was* you!"

"I hope I didn't hurt any of you." Herdlip looked sad, scared and sorry all at once. "When I changed, I felt so hungry . . . I could hardly control myself. I ate raw meat and rotten fish – *urgh!*" His legs wobbled, and he flopped to the grimy dungeon floor.

Gipsy crouched beside him. "What happened? What made you change like that?"

"An unlucky accident," said Herdlip miserably. "I tried to cure myself with

the chemicals you brought from the
ship, but it's no good. I have changed
twice now. When I change again it
will be for the last time, and I'll stay
a meat-eating monster for ever." He
closed his eyes. "You see, I didn't just
come here to cure King Jeck of
Ribchomper's Mump-Bumps. I came
here to cure him of being a *carnivore!*"

Teggs stared. "What do you mean?"

Herdlip lifted his chin proudly. "I
have created a potion called

Herbicarnus-X," he explained. "This miracle of medicine turns any meat-eater who drinks it into a plant-eater! It doesn't work straight away – the body can fight off the transformation at first. But after three changes, that's it. The carnivore becomes a herbivore and stays that way!" He shrugged. "When I was asked to cure King Jeck, it seemed like the perfect opportunity to test my potion."

"You wanted to turn King Jeck into a plant-eater?" Teggs looked baffled. "But why? His subjects would turn against him on the spot!"

Herdlip looked excited. "No, they wouldn't. Because once the change is complete, the new plant-eater is left full

of special Herbicarnus-X germs –
harmless to him, but very, very
infectious. Every carnivore he meets
will catch them!"

"So then *they* will turn into plant-
eaters too," Gipsy realized, "and go on
spreading the infection . . ."

"The change will spread like wildfire,"
Herdlip agreed. "It will even spread
through space to other meat-eater
worlds." His eyes gleamed. "Imagine
it, my friends! No more ravenous-
raptor invasions. No more T. rex terror
raids . . . Plant-eaters need never fear
carnivores again – for soon they will
cease to exist and we shall have
everlasting peace!"

Teggs shook his head sadly. "We all
want peace, Herdlip, but not like this.
Different dinosaurs have different
natures. We have to learn to live
together – not wipe each other out!"

"But don't you see?" Herdlip looked

puzzled. "I'm not hurting anyone, only *changing* them."

Iggy glared at him. "But carnivore worlds are pretty much plant-free – *meat*-eaters don't need them. So what are all your instant herbivores going to feed on?"

Herdlip frowned. "Er, I hadn't thought of that."

"Most of them will starve!" Teggs realized with horror. "Even if we give them food from our planets, there's not nearly enough for everyone."

"Captain!" Gipsy clapped her hoofs together with relief. "It's OK. Herdlip didn't give his potion to the real King Jeck, remember? It was Prince Poota in disguise!"

Herdlip's face fell. "It was?"

Gipsy nodded "And since Poota isn't really sick, why would he bother to drink that potion?"

"Of course!" said Teggs with relief. "So it looks like the only dino changing around here is you, Herdlip. But how come? You said it was an accident . . ."

Herdlip shrugged helplessly. "I was just mixing an extra-strong batch of Herbicarnus-X potion in the *Sauropod* lab, when we were attacked. The ship lurched sideways, and the potion splashed all over me. And though I perfected it to turn meat-eaters into harmless herbivores, it seems it does the opposite too – it turns plant-eaters into savage, crazy *carnivores!*"

Gipsy gasped in horror. "Does that

95

mean that when you change for the third time, you will spread the germs and turn all of *us* into carnivores too?" Herdlip nodded.

Iggy gulped. "We could infect the whole Vegetarian Sector."

"And turn every peaceful plant-eater into a raging monster!" Teggs groaned. "Your insane plan has backfired, Herdlip. Never mind the Mump-Bumps – this is the *true* Carnivore Curse!"

"I-I didn't mean for things to turn out this way," wailed Herdlip. "You must lock me up all alone somewhere for ever, so no one else will catch my germs."

"We will find doctors who might

be able to make you well again," Teggs told him. "But first you *must* cure the real King Jeck. There's not a moment to lose!"

Gipsy frowned. "Wait a sec. What happened to Donkle?"

"Griffen conked him on the head and he fell over . . ." Iggy scratched his chin. "Hey! He's gone!"

"He must have woken up and sneaked off when we weren't looking," Teggs realized. "And that means he's on his way to warn Prince Poota!"

"No, my dear Captain!" A new voice echoed out commandingly. "It means he has *already* warned me! I've been listening to Herdlip's explanations with great interest . . ."

A hunched figure, wrapped up in blankets and clutching hot-water bottles, swept in through the dungeon doorway, followed by eight baryonyx guards.

"Escape through the sewers, Captain!" Iggy raised his fists. "I'll delay them for as long as I can!"

But the guards pulled out their guns.
With a dozen ray-blasts they knocked
rocks from the wall behind them,
causing a cave-in that blocked off the
sewer tunnel. Herdlip squeaked and
held up his hands – Teggs, Gipsy and
Iggy reluctantly did the same.

Now the swaddled figure straightened

up to his full, imposing height. He
shrugged off the blankets and tossed
the squelchy rubber bottles to the
ground. His swollen face looked like
someone had inflated it with a bicycle
pump – but then he spat on his hands
and wiped off the mumpy-bumpy
disguise to reveal cruel, aristocratic
croc-like features underneath.

"Just when we thought things couldn't get any worse," breathed Gipsy. "Here he is at last – Prince Poota."

Teggs nodded grimly. "And it seems he's got us well and truly trapped!"

Chapter Nine

SPLASH IT ALL OVER

"Hi, fans!" Poota said with a cheesy grin. "Yes, it's me – Prince Pellito Poota. But perhaps you'd prefer to call me Soon-to-be-*King* Pellito Poota, the priceless pin-up who'll make all plant-eaters perish!"

"How about we call you Putrid Prince Poopy-Pants?" Iggy suggested.

Teggs nodded. "You looked better with your make-up on."

"Aha, but I have changed my plans," said Poota triumphantly, "now that I know about Herdlip's *monster* problem."

"How did you find out?" demanded Iggy.

"Dear, devoted Donkle has a secret microphone hidden up his nostril," Poota explained. "Thanks to him I've overheard every word you've said – you could say that I *nose* everything!" His little joke was met with silence. Poota flashed a warning look at the guards, and they quickly burst out laughing. "That's better."

"Where *is* Donkle, anyway?" asked Gipsy.

"On his way to the royal bedchamber," Poota replied. "Now his head's feeling better, he can help to guard my sickly uncle – along with that idiot Griffen and your friend Arx."

"Oh, no," Teggs groaned. "You heard me tell Arx to take King Jeck and Griffen back to Herdlip's bedroom, didn't you?"

"And my guards captured all three
of them the moment they appeared!"
Poota chuckled. "But it is your own
fate that should concern you. King Jeck
is nearly dead, and I shall soon be
king. My first act will be to send you
back home full of Herbicarnus-X — so
that all veggie dinos will mutate into
mindless, meat-guzzling monsters!"

"We haven't caught Herdlip's rotten
germs yet," said Iggy defiantly.

"And *I* haven't drunk that potion he
gave me," Poota retorted, pulling the
beaker from a pouch on his belt. "So

I'm going to splash it all over the three of you instead. It will change you just as it has changed him."

The astrosaurs looked at each other helplessly.

"By wiping all plant-eaters from the face of the Jurassic Quadrant, I shall become the greatest carnivore king in all history," breathed Poota. He did a little dance in excitement. "My praises shall be sung from Raptos to Teerex Major. I bet I'll even be voted Most Dashing Meat-Muncher of the year!"

"I doubt it," said Teggs. "As far as I can see, you're just a big *drip*!"

With that, the six-ton stegosaurus suddenly leaped through the air and landed on a pile of

Poota's discarded hot-water bottles. The plugs popped out and water slooshed through the air, drenching Poota completely. He spluttered in outrage and slipped over onto his bum.

At the same moment, while

Herdlip cowered in a corner, Iggy and Gipsy burst into action.

Iggy pounced on two of the guards and banged their heads together, while Gipsy knocked down three more baryonyx with some dynamic dino-judo jabs.

Teggs curled up and rolled about the dungeon like a spiky, self-propelled wrecking ball, scattering the remaining guards.

"Let's get out of here!" he shouted.

Iggy and Gipsy hustled Herdlip out

of the dungeon and rushed after Teggs
through the dark stone corridors.

"We must get to the *Sauropod* and
take off," Herdlip cried, scurrying along
behind the others.

"Not without Arx," said Iggy flatly,
and Gipsy nodded.

"Besides, our mission was to make
King Jeck well again," Teggs puffed. He
could already hear dozens of heavy
footfalls behind them as Poota and his
guards gave chase. "We *must* get to the
king's bedchamber – Prince Poota kept
your potion, Herdlip. Perhaps he still
has those tablets you gave him."

"But now Jeck is a prisoner too,"
Gipsy reminded him. "Along with Arx
and Griffen!"

"So let's set them free!" Teggs skidded
to a halt, pointing down a side passage.
"Look! The royal bedroom is through
those golden double doors. Let's surprise
any guards waiting inside . . ."

Teggs, Iggy and Gipsy ran at top
speed, ready to shoulder-charge the
heavy doors. But just as the astrosaurs
were about to hit them, the doors were
pulled open!

"*Whooaaaaaa!*" All three of them
lost their balance and went tumbling
into the smoky room, finishing up
in a tangled heap on the floor.

Teggs noticed Herdlip's
little pillbox lying
beside a solid-gold
hat stand, forgotten
on the floor. If he
could only reach it . . .

"Don't move, twig-gobblers." Teggs
glanced back and saw Sergeant Donkle
sniggering in the
doorway, holding
Herdlip in a neck-
lock and waving
a communicator.
"Poota warned
me you'd escaped.
He said to me
you might come
here, so I was
ready to trick
you."

"Captain!" cried a familiar voice.

Teggs looked to his left – and saw
Arx being held at gunpoint by four

more guards. On the king's grand bed,
Jeck and Griffen lay tied up and
helpless, both staring angrily at Teggs.

"Donkle told us that Herdlip's
'special herbal drink' is a poisonous
potion that turns any carnivore into a
plant-eater," hissed Griffen.

"Can this be true?" croaked Jeck.

"I'm afraid so," said Teggs quietly.
"But I promise, we didn't know."

"A likely story!" Prince Poota stood
dripping in the doorway, eight slightly

111

battered guards just behind him. "But who cares? The important thing is, Herdlip's potion works the other way round too."

"It's true," moaned Herdlip bitterly. "Twice now, I've turned into a carnivore – and when the third change comes, I will remain that way for ever."

"Indeed." Poota chuckled and pulled out his flask of Herbicarnus-X. "In the meantime, one splash of this will soon turn Captain *Dregs* and his boring buddies into savage, bone-crunching beasts as well!" He pulled out the cork. "Prepare to kiss your plant-eating past goodbye, astrosaurs! You'll soon be eating *each other*!"

Chapter Ten

THE END OF THE CURSE

"*Wait!*" Herdlip shouted, clutching at his throat. A cloud of green smoke burst from his bottom, and Donkle fell back, choking.

"Oh, help! It–it's starting to happen . . . the final change!"

"The point of no return," said Teggs grimly. "No need to splash us now, Poota — we will all catch Herdlip's carnivore germs anyway!"

Arx's guards and those behind Poota pointed their guns at Herdlip, but the prince shook his head. "Don't shoot him yet," he hissed. "Wait till he has fully transformed. Let the plant-eaters behold the fate that awaits them and all their kind!"

Astrosaurs and baryonyx alike stared in horrified amazement as the terrifying transformation took hold. Herdlip's purple scales turned green. He reared up on his back legs as his body inflated and his head turned spiky. His teeth and claws grew long and pointed, and his eyes began to glow.

Arx pulled away from his incredulous guards and threw himself at Poota's feet. "Please, great Prince, I beg you," he moaned. "Don't let me change into a monster! Let me be your slave instead."

"Arx!" Teggs frowned. "Pull yourself together!"

"I'll do anything, sweet Poota," Arx went on. "Save me!"

"Ha!" Poota sneered down at the trembling triceratops. "See how this weakling pleads with me for his life!"

"Yep," Arx agreed. "This 'weakling' just needed to get close enough to do *this*!"

And suddenly, in a blur of horns and hoofs, he butted Poota in the stomach and snatched the potion away! Poota staggered backward, tripped over the still-choking Donkle and crashed into his guards, knocking most of them to the floor.

The startled guards still standing

aimed their ray-guns at Arx. "Don't think so!" Teggs shouted, and whacked the nearest baryonyx with his spiky tail. Iggy punched another, and Gipsy high-kicked the other two clear over the bed! They landed in a heap at the back of the room.

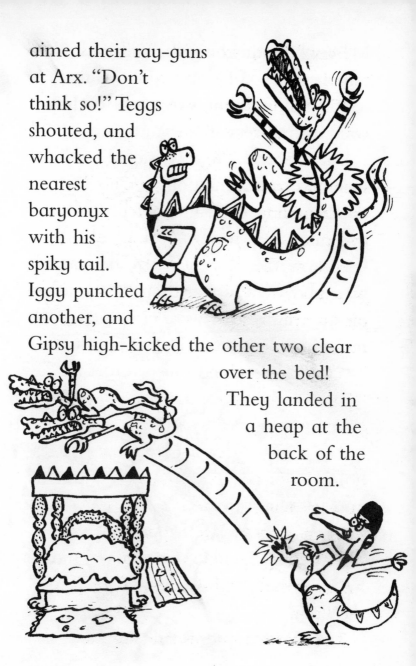

Meanwhile, clutching the precious potion to his chest, Arx took on the rest of Poota's guards in horn-to-claw combat and sent them scattering.

But a horrifying howl signalled that Herdlip's transformation was now complete. The mild-mannered dinosaur had become a towering, snarling, spitting terror. His eyes were fiery red, his claws were longer than ever, and his cavernous jaws were crammed with flesh-shredding teeth. He roared at the astrosaurs, searching out a target.

Then he lunged towards Arx . . .

"Look out!" Teggs cried. "Herdlip can't control himself any longer!"

The monster's mouth stretched wide ready to bite the triceratops – and Arx sloshed the contents of the flask inside! With a spluttering roar, Herdlip broke off his attack and reeled across the room. He stuck out his green tongue and belched like a foghorn. His scaly skin turned first blue, then orange, then livid red, smoking as if he was burning inside.

"What's happening?" Gipsy shouted, dodging Herdlip's flailing tail.

"Keep away from him," Arx yelled back, watching in fascination.

"I wish I could!" Teggs said, as Herdlip stamped a spiky foot mere millimetres from the little pillbox. "But if I don't get the King's *real* medicine right now it could be too late!"

Teggs dived over the monster's thrashing tail and did a forward roll, grabbing for the tiny container. But Herdlip's other foot slammed down beside Teggs's head, and the shock waves knocked the box further away.

Teggs slithered after it, but the belching, bellowing creature kicked Jeck's solid gold hat-stand over.

CLUNK! It hit Teggs on the head. The room began to spin around him. Desperately, he stretched out his arm, groping blindly . . . and grasped the pillbox just as Herdlip picked him up and hurled him across the room.

"I've heard of flying doctors, but this is ridiculous!" Teggs cried, opening the pillbox as he zoomed through the air. "Your Majesty, quick – open wide!"

And just as he sailed over Jeck's bed, Teggs dropped two tablets down the king's throat! With an astonished gurgle, the

old baryonyx swallowed them.

"Quick, catch the captain!" Iggy shouted to Arx.

"I think Prince Poota and his guards are going to catch him," said Arx. "And for once, that's a *good* thing!"

Sure enough, Teggs had a soft landing on top of Poota, Donkle and half a dozen other guards. After a muffled chorus of *OOF!*s the baryonyx baddies could say no more.

"Look at Herdlip!" Gipsy cried suddenly. "He's changed back to normal!"

"She's right!" said Iggy. Herdlip was still steaming and hiccupping a bit, but was his old, small, sellosaurus self again.

Teggs stared at Arx. "Did you know that would happen?"

"You heard Poota, Captain." Arx was looking pleased with himself. "Herdlip invented Herbicarnus-X to turn carnivores into plant-eaters."

Gipsy got his meaning. "And it was only when Herdlip changed for the third and final time that his carnivore condition became permanent."

"Exactly!" Arx smiled. "I gambled that once he became a *true* carnivore, another dose of Herbicarnus-X would shock his system back to normal. All we have to do now is keep him tucked away until we're sure he is completely cured!"

"Brilliant!" Iggy helped Herdlip back up. "How are you feeling?"

"I'm feeling sorry," said Herdlip. He waddled up to Griffen and Jeck, and quickly untied their ropes. "Truly, very sorry. I realize now what a terrible thing I nearly did."

"Too right, you snivelling stem-nibbler!" Griffen grabbed Herdlip angrily by the arm. "You think saying sorry can make things better?"

"N-n-n-no," Herdlip stammered. "But for starters, I will share my cure for Ribchomper's Mump-Bumps with all meat-eaters, free of charge – so no carnivore will ever suffer from this dreadful illness again."

"That is a kind offer, Herdlip," King Jeck declared, sitting up with a faint sparkle in his eyes. "Your cure is certainly good stuff, I feel much better already! Do put him down, Griffen."

"Yes, Your Majesty." Griffen bowed

his head and let Herdlip go.

Teggs felt something wriggle under his bottom and lifted a cheek. It was Poota. "No uncle, you must destroy them!" he pleaded. "They planned to change us into plant-eating pansies. They planned to wipe out our way of life."

"Only *one* plant-eater planned to do that," Jeck declared. "Just as only one baryonyx – you, Poota – planned to do the same to them." He looked at Teggs and his astrosaurs and nodded. "I shall never forget how bravely you've all fought to put things right."

Teggs saluted him. "Admiral Rosso and the entire Dinosaur Space Service will be very pleased to know you're getting better."

"And now I shall arrange for two more ships to escort you safely back to your own side of space." Jeck sighed. "It seems that both our peoples have centuries of hate and mistrust to overcome before there can ever be peace."

"True." Teggs smiled. "But with wise rulers like you around, perhaps one day it *will* happen."

"As someone who's been both a plant-eater and a carnivore, from now on I'm going to do all I can to *make* that happen!" Dr Herdlip declared.

Griffen nodded. "And I am going to make sure that Poota and his team of traitors are sent to the smelliest dungeons on the whole planet." He smiled nastily. "As soon as I've upheld a very important baryonyx tradition, that is. Captain Teggs, if you would excuse me?"

Teggs climbed off Poota and stood
back – allowing Griffen to conk the
fallen prince on the head with his tail.
With a dizzy groan, Poota sank back
to the floor.

Jeck beamed approvingly. "That's
my annoying nephew sent off to
dreamland."

"With his dreams of being the
perfect king well and truly over,"
Arx added.

"And now that we've cured two
different kinds of Carnivore Curse in

one day," said Teggs, "I think it's time we also healed the Herbivore Hunger."

Gipsy, Iggy and Arx gave him puzzled smiles. "The *what*?"

"It's a desperate need I often get for a brand-new, super-exciting adventure!" Teggs grinned at his friends. "Luckily, with a crew like you, a ship like the *Sauropod* and a crazy cosmos like ours, I know that the perfect cure is never far away — so let's go and find it!"

THE END